3

Ollie Ostrich was the first person she met. He was strutting across the grassland. Although Ollie was a bird he did not fly, but he could run very fast on his long legs.

"Ollie, you have a long neck like my Geoffrey. Please can you tell me what you do when you get a sore throat?"

Ollie was a show-off. He tossed his head saying, "Me? I never get a sore throat". Then away he ran, fanning out his tail feathers in his usual showy manner.

Further along the track Greta met Adam and Amanda Ape. They were called chimpanzees, and were very clever acrobats.

Before Greta was able to ask them about sore throats, they dashed off to continue their game of 'Tag' chasing through the tree tops.

They scampered up the trunk of a nearby tree, swinging from branch to branch and then from tree to tree.

Greta was afraid for them. She thought that they must surely fall but, of course, they never did.

GEOFFREY'S
SORE THROAT

Reprinted October 1995

ISBN: 1 872547 15 X

Text© Maria Sutherland 1990
Illustrations© T J C Walsh 1990

Published by Sherbourne Publications
Sweeney Mountain, Oswestry
Shropshire SY10 9EX, UK
Tel: 01691 657853

Set in 18/25 Plantin

Typesetting and Origination by K C Graphics Limited

Printed by Clarkeprint Ltd.
45-47 Stour Street, Ladywood, Birmingham B18 7AJ.
Tel: 0121-454 7117

GEOFFREY'S
SORE THROAT

by
Maria Sutherland
Illustrated by T J C Walsh

To Dropmore School

Best Wishes

Maria Sutherland

April '96.

Sherbourne Publications

Geoffrey, the baby giraffe, was not at all well when his mother, Greta, went to wake him for his breakfast. He had a sore throat.

Geoffrey had a very, very, very sore throat because he had such a long, long, long neck. Greta did not know what to do about it and so she went to ask her neighbours for their help.

"Now you stay there until I get back", she told Geoffrey.

Mhina, a boy from the village volunteered to stay with him until Greta returned.

She walked down towards the river and found some of her neighbours there.

First, standing up to his chin in the river, there was Hector Hippopotamus.

Greta called to him, but Hector opened his mouth and gave a large yawn, as though life was all so very tiresome. He looked at her with his little piggy eyes, then disappeared to go for a walk along the bottom of the river.

"Sometimes, he can be so rude", Greta said to herself.

Then there was Cora Crocodile who lay on the river bank, at the edge of the water, pretending to be asleep.

Cora was never very friendly. Most of the animals kept well away from Cora, and Greta decided not to disturb her.

Cora's cousin, Charlie Crocodile, was also pretending to be asleep but he was grinning and showing his many sharp teeth.

Greta left them both well alone and went on her way.

Ellie Elephant was gathering up water with her trunk to wash Emily, her baby when Greta found her.

"Geoffrey has a sore throat Ellie, whatever can I do to make him better?" asked Greta.

"Well, I can't really help you, Greta, because we don't get sore throats only very, very, very, dry trunks and water is good for them".

Ellie then carried on spraying her baby with water. Emily, like all babies, enjoyed being bathed.

13

Poor Greta was very worried, no-one seemed to be able to help. The trail she was following went past a large tree. In the shade of this tree Zena Zebra and her foal Zoe, were grazing.

"Zena, can you please tell me what I can do to make my Geoffrey's sore throat better?"

"Yes, of course, Greta. What you need is a warm woollen scarf. I don't know where you will find one though, but Lucy Lioness might know. She is with her cubs by the water hole".

On her way Greta spotted Sidney Snake sunning himself on a rock.

"Sidney, please can you tell me where I can find a woollen scarf?"

Sidney did not answer for a long time. When he did, he slowly raised his head, looked at Greta through cold, steely eyes and hissed rudely, "How should I know?"

Then, silently, he slithered away and disappeared behind the rocks.

Leo Lion and Lucy Lioness were about to take their cubs for a walk when Greta found them.

"You are both very clever," said Greta. "Do you know where I can find a woollen scarf? My Geoffrey has a very, very, very, sore throat and a scarf might help to cure it".

They shook their great heads, sadly. "You go home to Geoffrey", said Lucy kindly. "We will see what our friends can do. A meeting of all the animals will be called".

Victor Vulture was very helpful that day. He flew around telling all the animals that Leo and Lucy wanted them at a meeting.

Everyone gathered in a clearing and Lucy told them the problem. "What is to be done about Geoffrey's sore throat? He needs a woollen scarf to help him get better".

There was silence. No one spoke up at all.

"Come on now, think hard", said Lucy, "there must be something we can do to help".

No-one said anything, but they were all thinking hard.

To everyone's surprise, Sidney Snake, that slippery fellow who was nobody's friend, slid through to the front of the group.

"I have an idea", he hissed. "You and Leo have very thick coats. You could shake yourselves and shed some of your fur. I could slither through the swamp until I become a sticky snake. Then, when I am muddy all over, I could roll in your fur and become a scarf for Geoffrey".

Everyone thought it was a wonderful idea.

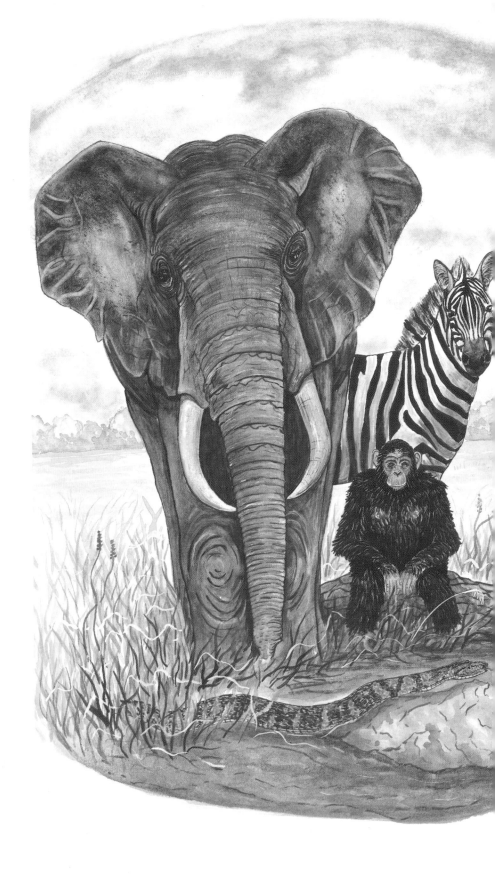

23

When Greta arrived home, Mhina was still sitting beside poor Geoffrey. Greta told them why she had been away so long.

"Leo and Lucy Lion are calling a meeting of all the animals to see what can be done".

Mhina said, "When I get a sore throat my mother has some special syrup for it. I will go and ask her for some".

When Mhina came back with the syrup he gave Geoffrey a large spoonful. Mhina's mother had also sent a blanket to keep Geoffrey warm.

When the animals went to tell Greta of their plan, she was delighted and Mhina said, "It is the best idea I have ever heard".

Leo and Lucy shook themselves until there was a pile of golden fur on the ground. Sidney Snake, now a sticky snake, rolled over and over in the pile of fur.

Sidney soon looked more like a big, cuddly, woolly caterpillar than a snake. Then Sidney wound himself round and round Geoffrey's long neck.

"This is good, it's so lovely and warm", Geoffrey managed to croak.

That night everyone slept close by, waiting to see whether Geoffrey's sore throat would be cured.

By morning Geoffrey could speak. His very, very, very sore throat was completely better. The syrup which Mhina's mother had sent was good medicine and the warm blanket helped. But it was really Sidney's new fur coat which had cured Geoffrey's sore throat by keeping his long, long, long neck warm.

Everyone agreed that Sidney Snake was a very good fellow. They all wanted to feel his fur coat just to see how warm and soft it felt.

The sun was hot and Sidney Snake began to feel very uncomfortable. He could no longer slide along the ground.

"Please can someone help me to get rid of my fur coat, I cannot slither along and I am so hot".

Hector Hippopotamus let Sidney curl up on his large head and carried him down to the river. Geoffrey, Greta, Mhina and all their animal friends went too.

Hector waded in until his head was level with the water. Then Sidney Snake went for a swim, to wash off his fur coat.

When Sidney was clean again, Hector Hippopotamus and Sidney Snake returned to the river bank where their friends were waiting. Sidney then slid onto his favourite rock and dried himself in the sun.

Sidney was a hero and he was having a lovely time. He enjoyed being friends with all his neighbours, at least for today.

Mhina went for a walk with Geoffrey to show him where the smaller trees were.

"Eat the young leaves from the top, Geoffrey, they will help you to grow big and strong like other giraffes", Mhina told him.

Greta was pleased that all her neighbours had been friendly towards each other for once and it was all because her Geoffrey had had a very, very, very sore throat.